TEENAGE MUTANT NINJA TURTLES™

Lean, Green Smackdown Machine!

by Steve Murphy

illustrated by Aristides Ruiz and Mike Giles

Simon Spotlight

New York London Toronto Sydney

D0117317

Based on the TV series *Teenage Mutant Ninja Turtles*™ as seen on Fox and Cartoon Network™

SIMON SPOTLIGHT

An imprint of Simon & Schuster Children's Publishing Division

1230 Avenue of the Americas, New York, New York 10020

10 9 8 7 6 5 4 3

ISBN 0-689-87059-0

"My sons, what is the reason for all this noise?" asked Splinter.

"Just Michelangelo and Raphael wrestling for the TV remote," Leonardo answered.

"They're wrestling to see who controls which wrestling show they watch," said Donatello. "Wrestling over *wrestling*!"

Just then a TV commercial caught everyone's attention.

"You heard me right, wrestling fan," said the man. "An amateur wrestling match. Tonight at the Ronald Rump Civic Center. Open to everyone and anyone."

Then with a smirk the man added, "Anyone with enough *guts.* Do *you* have enough guts, wrestling fan?"

"We've got the guts!" Raphael shouted.

"And the *skillingest* skills!" added Michelangelo. "Piece of cake, bro!"

"Yeah, we're there!" agreed Raphael. "Now all we have to do is come up with some costumes."

"Get ready to rumble!" they both yelled.

Michelangelo and Raphael quickly came up with their wrestling outfits and headed to the Ronald Rump Civic Center.

"I like your look, boys," said Lon Jing, the wrestling promoter. "Sorta mutant, sorta turtle, definitely green. Green and lean. I've got it: the Lean, Green Machine!"

"How about . . . the Lean, Green Smackdown Machine?" asked Michelangelo.

"Even better," answered Mr. Jing. "Now follow me."

Mr. Jing led the two brothers into the wrestling arena.
"I'm pumped!" said Raphael when he saw the huge crowd.
"Me too!" Michelangelo said. "This is way cooler than seeing it on TV!"

In the ring the referee introduced the wrestlers. "In this corner, weighing more than most automobiles, are two brothers—Hun and Ahnold—the human avalanches otherwise known as . . . the Massive Man-Mountains!"

"And in this corner," he said, pointing to the two Turtles, "looking fit and mean . . . the Lean, Green Smackdown Machine!"

"Uh-oh," Michelangelo whispered to Raphael, "the guy with the beard is Shredder's right-hand man, Hun!"

The bell rang, and suddenly Hun and Ahnold had the Turtles up in the air! "Looks like a double twirly bird, folks," said the referee. "The Massive Man-Mountains are playing helicopter with the Smackdown Machine, both of whom are beginning to look a little too green, if you know what I mean."

Crack!

Raphael and Michelangelo struck each other—hard.

"That had to hurt, ladies and gentlemen," said the referee.

"Ha. Was that not fun, my brother?" said Hun, laughing.

"Ha. Big fun, my brother," Ahnold replied. "Come, let us have more fun with these little green men."

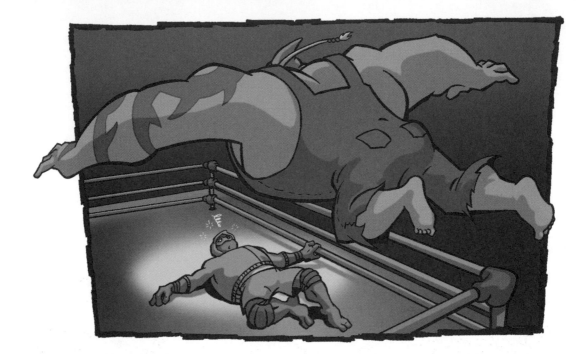

Michelangelo and Raphael kept getting pounded by Hun and Ahnold.

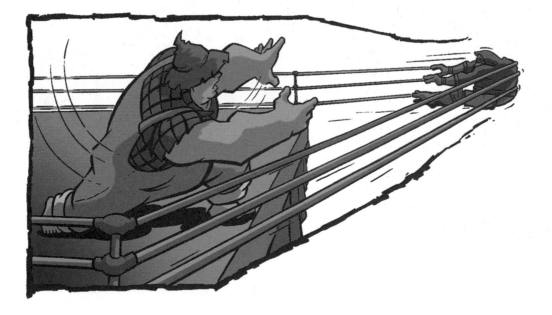

Raphael groaned. "We need a plan, Mikey. We're getting our butts kicked."

"Too bad ninjitsu isn't allowed in wrestling," moaned Michelangelo.

Suddenly Raphael had an idea. "You're right, Mikey!" he exclaimed. "We can't use ninjitsu, but we *can* use another form of our ninja training. Come on, get up."

"Look," Raphael whispered, "we can use one of Splinter's lessons: 'Turn your enemy's size and strength to your advantage.' Remember that one?"

"Right! We can turn their size and strength *against each other*!" Michelangelo whispered back.

With a loud scream—"HAI-YA!"—the two Turtles leaped toward their opponents.

"Hey, no fair, little man," said Ahnold as he tripped over Michelangelo.

"All's fair in love and war . . . and wrestling," said Raphael, making the same move on Hun.

"On the count of three," said the referee. "One."
"I cannot move," Ahnold said to Hun. "Get off me, my brother."
"Two," counted off the referee.
"I cannot move," said Hun. "These little men are holding us down."
"Three!" yelled the referee.

"And the winners are . . . the Lean, Green Smackdown Machine!" proclaimed the referee. The crowd cheered wildly.

"Check out this cool trophy belt," Raphael crowed.

"Cowabunga!" Michelangelo yelled to the crowd.

A short while later the two Turtles made their way home.

"We watched you guys on TV," said Donatello. "You had us worried for a while there."

"Excellent trophy," Leonardo said, "but it makes me wonder."

"Wonder what?" Raphael asked.

"It makes me wonder who will be wearing it," said Leonardo.

Raphael and Michelangelo looked at each other.

"I will," Raphael declared.

"No," said Michelangelo, "I will."

"Then get ready to rumble," Raphael told Michelangelo.

Just then Splinter entered the room. "Now what is the reason for the noise this time?" he asked.

"Just Michelangelo and Raphael wrestling again," Leonardo replied.

"*Now* they're wrestling to see who gets to wear their wrestling belt," said Donatello. "Always wrestling over wrestling."

"Ah, but at least this time *we* have the remote, my sons," Splinter said,
turning on a Bruce Lee movie.